Translated by Anthea Bell

SANDY CREEK and the distinctive Sandy Creek logo are registered trademarks of Barnes & Noble, Inc.

Copyright © 1989 by Max Velthuijs Foundation

First published in Great Britain in 1989 by Andersen Press Ltd., London
This 2015 edition published by Sandy Creek.

ISBN 978-1-4351-5750-7

Manufactured by Tien Wah Press in Malaysia
Lot #:
2 4 6 8 10 9 7 5 3 1
01/15

Frog
in Love

Hope you enjoy
this "lovey" story.
Happy ♡ Day!
Gammie and Grampa
2/15

Max Velthuijs

Frog was sitting on the river bank.
He felt funny. He didn't know if he was happy
or sad.

He had been walking around in a dream all week.
What could be wrong with him?

Then he met Pig.

"Hello, Frog," said Pig. "You don't look very well. What's the matter with you?"

"I don't know," said Frog. "I feel like laughing and crying at the same time. And there's something going thump-thump inside me, here."

"Maybe you've caught a cold," said Pig.
"You'd better go home to bed."
Frog went on his way. He was worried.

Then he passed Hare's house.

"Hare," he said, "I don't feel well."

"Come on in and sit down," said Hare, kindly.

"Now then," said Hare, "what's the matter with you?"

"Sometimes I go hot, and sometimes I go cold,"
said Frog, "and there's something going thump-thump
inside me, here." And he put his hand on his chest.

Hare thought hard, just like a real doctor.

"I see," he said. "It's your heart. Mine goes thump-thump too."

"But mine sometimes thumps faster than usual," said Frog.

"It goes one-two, one-two, one-two."

Hare took a big book down from his bookshelf and
turned the pages. "Aha!" he said. "Listen to this. Heartbeat,
sped up, hot and cold turns . . . it means you're in love!"

"In love?" said Frog, surprised. "Wow! I'm in love!"

And he was so pleased that he did a tremendous jump,

right out of the door and up in the air.

Pig was quite scared when Frog suddenly came falling
from the sky.
"You seem to be better," said Pig.
"I am! I feel just fine," said Frog. "I'm in love!"
"Well, that's good news. Who are you in love with?"
asked Pig. Frog hadn't stopped to think about that.

"I know!" he said. "I'm in love with the pretty, nice, lovely white duck!"
"You can't be," said Pig. "A frog can't be in love with a duck. You're green and she's white."
But Frog didn't let that bother him.

He couldn't write, but he could make beautiful paintings. Back at home he painted a lovely picture, with red and blue and lots of green, his favorite color.

In the evening, when it was dark, he went out
with his picture and pushed it under the door
of Duck's house.
His heart was beating hard with excitement.

Duck was very surprised when she found the picture.
"Who could have sent me this beautiful picture?"
she cried, and she hung it on the wall.

The next day Frog picked a beautiful bunch of flowers.
He was going to give them to Duck.
But when he reached her door, he felt too shy to face
her. He put the flowers down on the doorstep and ran
away as fast as he could.
And so it went on, day after day.
Frog just couldn't muster up the courage to speak to Duck.

Duck was very pleased with all her lovely presents.
But who could be sending them?

Poor Frog!
He didn't enjoy his food anymore, and he couldn't
sleep at night.
Things went on like this for weeks.

How could he show Duck he loved her?
"I must do something nobody else can do," he decided.
"I must break the world high jump record! Dear Duck
will be very surprised, and then she'll love me back."

Frog started training at once.
He practiced the high jump for days on end.
He jumped higher and higher, right up to the clouds.
No frog in the world had ever jumped so high before.

"What could be the matter with Frog?" asked Duck, worried. "Jumping like that is dangerous. He's going to hurt himself."
She was right.

At thirteen minutes past two on Friday afternoon, things went wrong. Frog was doing the highest jump in history when he lost his balance and fell to the ground.
Duck, who happened to be passing by at the time, came hurrying up to help him.

Frog could hardly walk. Supporting him carefully, Duck took him home with her. She nursed him with tender loving care.

"Oh, Frog, you could have been killed!" she said. "You really must be careful. I'm so fond of you!"

And then, at last, Frog found his courage.

"I'm very fond of you too, dear Duck," he stammered. His heart was going thump-thump faster than ever, and his face turned deep green.

Ever since then, they have loved each other dearly.
A frog and a duck . . .
Green and white.
Love knows no boundaries.